Bella Sara™

2

Valkrist's Flight

HarperCollins®, 🐎®, and Harper Festival®
are trademarks of HarperCollins Publishers.

Bella Sara: Valkrist's Flight
Cover and interior illustrations by Spoops
Copyright © 2009 Hidden City Games, Inc. © 2005–2008 conceptcard. All rights reserved.
BELLA SARA is a trademark of conceptcard and is used by Hidden City Games under license.
Licensed by Granada Ventures Limited.
Printed in the United States of America.
For information address HarperCollins Children's Books,
a division of HarperCollins Publishers,
10 East 53rd Street, New York, NY 10022.
www.harpercollinschildrens.com
www.bellasara.com

Library of Congress catalog card number: 2008924830
ISBN 978-0-06-167330-6
◆
First Edition

09 10 11 12 13 CG/CW 10 9 8 7 6 5

Valkrist's Flight

Written by Felicity Brown
Illustrated by Spoops

HarperFestival®
A Division of HarperCollinsPublishers

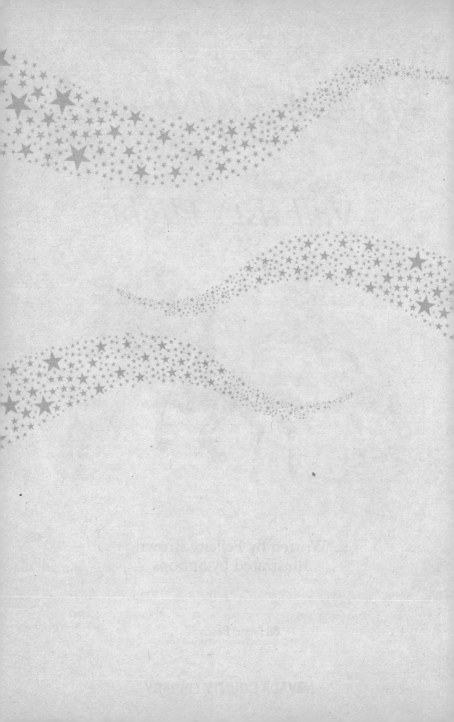

$\mathscr{E}$mma Roland woke soon after sunrise.

Before she opened her eyes, the eleven-year-old girl let her dream linger. She held on to her memory of the smell of her mother cooking breakfast in the kitchen, and the sound of her father knocking on her bedroom door. "Emma, the horses need us," her father had said.

He used to say that every morning. Even now, in her dreams, her father's voice had woken Emma up and reminded her about the horses they both loved. Even now, after he—

Emma opened her eyes, staring up at the rafters. Her mother had always told her keeping busy would help her stop thinking about something unpleasant. So Emma pulled off her covers, jumping into action.

She wasn't in her old bedroom— she now slept in the hayloft in the stable at Day Mare Ranch. Emma had cleaned up the loft and made it a cozy sanctuary.

Hearing her feet on the loft's floorboards, the horses beneath her snuffled, expecting their breakfast. "I'll be right there," Emma called, as she twisted her hair in a loose braid.

Emma had been sleeping in the hayloft for more than a month now. Emma never felt quite right unless the horses she adored were close by.

As she climbed down the loft's ladder, Emma had to admit that there was another reason she'd moved to the hayloft. When her aunt and uncle had taken over the Day Mare Ranch, her aunt Cynthia had redecorated the main house. It just didn't feel like the house Emma had grown up in anymore.

Emma was an only child, and two of her three cousins had gone off to college. Her youngest cousin, Colm, was just two years older than Emma, but he was so snotty that any day Emma didn't run into him was a good day.

The horses shuffled in their stalls as Emma walked down the stable's wide center aisle. There were twelve stalls in the barn, with a storage area under the loft, and an enclosed porch in the front near the tackroom and the wash bay. When Emma's father ran the ranch, all twelve stalls were usually occupied—with either the Quarter horses the ranch was renowned for breeding, or with boarded horses from other owners.

Now there were only six horses in the stable, along with Emma's Shetland pony, Mischief. Uncle Morgan wasn't as popular as her father, and many boarders had withdrawn their horses. The only remaining boarded horse was a black thoroughbred mare named Dowager.

Emma said hello to Mischief in the first stall. Mischief blinked up at Emma, fluttering his long eyelashes. The gold hoop earring in his ear glinted in a ray of sunlight, and Emma felt a swell of love for the adorable pony. Then she moved on to the horses.

"Good morning, Cookie," she told a proud chestnut stallion. He twitched his ears at her.

"Hello, Dewdrop," Emma greeted a young bay mare. Dewdrop nuzzled her gate—that was her way of asking for breakfast.

Blinky, a dark dapple mare with a white ghostlike shape on her forehead, craned her head as Emma approached. Emma patted her on her distinctive marking.

"Hey, Spaceship," Emma said soothingly to a gray, jittery yearling colt. Spaceship clopped in his stall, snorting. He was Blinky's son, but was much more high-strung.

The last family horse, Firelight, didn't look up as Emma arrived. Firelight was a dreamy mare and had been Emma's mother's favorite. But since the car accident—

Emma leaned into Firelight's stall and let out a sigh. "I miss her, too, Firelight," she said. Firelight twitched her legs, her enormous eyes so sad. "I'll have breakfast for you soon."

When Emma reached Dowager's stall, she was surprised to find the mare staring at her. Dowager's eyes twinkled . . . almost as though she were keeping a secret. . . .

Emma shook her head and got busy taking care of the horses. She removed all their blankets, and then she filled their troughs with fresh water. She gave them hay to eat.

After they were done eating, she checked their hooves. Cookie's shoes were still fine, but it was almost time for the farrier to come in for a trim.

Emma inspected the horses' tack to make sure all the equipment was in good shape. She slipped halters onto all the horses and walked Cookie, Dewdrop, and Blinky out to the corral so they could get some exercise. Uncle Morgan, Walt the stable foreman, and Brian the ranch hand would be along soon to start mucking out those horses' stalls. When they were done, Emma would bring the three back in, and then turn out Dowager, Firelight, Spaceship, and Mischief for their exercise.

While Cookie and Dewdrop trotted around the big dirt ring, Emma let herself relax. Watching horses run and play was her favorite pastime—horses were so easily joyful.

Dewdrop caught up to Cookie,

and for a moment they galloped side by side. Emma had an odd flash, a daydream so strong it was almost like a vision—the horses adorned in beautiful bridles, with magnificent saddles on their backs. They stepped smartly, fancy tassels fluttering on their heads. Emma saw them as royal horses, proud members of a powerful noble family—

"Emma!" a voice called behind her. She whirled around.

Walt strode out of the stable. "Working hard, or hardly working?" he snapped.

Emma bit her lip. Walt was always gruff, but he used to have an occasional kind word for her, recognizing how much she loved the horses. But since Uncle Morgan took over, everyone seemed to be in a bad mood.

"I'll watch the horses," Walt said. He nodded his head back toward the barn. "Go," he ordered. "Your uncle has something to ask you. *Now*, girl."

Hurrying back toward the stables, Emma racked her brain for anything she'd forgotten to do. Maybe she hadn't folded the blankets in the specific way he demanded. . . .

In the barn, Uncle Morgan had Dowager out in the front and was staring at the boarding thoroughbred mare with his fists on his hips.

Emma strode over to him. "Uncle Morgan," she panted, "is this about the blankets—?"

"Did you let Dowager out unsupervised?" Uncle Morgan interrupted, his eyes squinty. "Months ago?"

"N-no," Emma stammered, surprised. "Of course not. I would never—"

"You sure?" Uncle Morgan pressed. "Trying to save some time with your chores?"

Emma shook her head. "No, I'm sure," she replied. "Why?"

Her uncle sighed and ran his hand along Dowager's shiny black back.

"She's pregnant," he muttered darkly. "Dr. Dwyer just confirmed it. She wasn't when Miss Bridget boarded her with us."

Emma grimaced and reached out to rub Dowager's warm nose. "I didn't let her run free," she told him. "I wouldn't do that."

Uncle Morgan slapped Dowager's reins into Emma's hand. "Well, *someone* did," he barked. He screwed shut his eyes momentarily. "Take her in and give her a thorough grooming," he ordered. "Miss Bridget is not going to be happy. Our last boarder, too. This is a disaster. We can't afford—"

Before finishing his sentence, Uncle Morgan turned around and stormed toward the house. "Muck out the stalls while you're at it!" he called to his niece. "Alone! And make sure nothing like this *ever* happens again."

*E*mma didn't mind mucking out the stables. It was smelly work, but the horses needed fresh straw in their stalls or they'd get sick. What Emma *did* mind was being accused of something she hadn't done.

She worked out her anger by attacking the soiled straw, using her pitchfork to heave it into a wheelbarrow. Emma tried to block out Uncle Morgan's words, but they trickled into her brain anyway. Yes, it was terrible news that Dowager was pregnant . . . but that wasn't her fault. Emma's father had trusted her. If he were still alive—

Emma leaned on the fork's handle, blinking back tears. She wiped her cheek and glanced down the barn aisle to see if Brian the ranch hand had noticed.

Brian was busy working oil into a saddle. He glanced up and gave Emma a friendly wink.

Emma ducked her head, too upset to return Brian's greeting. More than anything, she wished her mother were there. Her mother had been able to explain how to handle unfair situations. With her parents gone, Emma felt like she didn't have a single person in the world who understood her completely.

Tearing up again, Emma scooped the straw with her pitchfork roughly, frustrated that she'd let herself think about things better left alone.

"Hello?" a young girl's voice called.

Emma turned around. In a

sunbeam stood a pretty, petite girl about her age. She gave Emma a friendly wave, and Emma leaned her pitchfork against the side of the stall.

The girl walked into the stables, and Emma saw that she was dressed in a formal riding outfit. She was wearing a black cap with dangling chin straps and a fitted black jacket. Her tall dress boots were shiny black, and her riding breeches were bright white. Emma glanced down at her own outfit. Her bib overalls and muck-covered boots suddenly seemed grimy.

As the girl passed Dowager's stall, she patted the black thoroughbred on the nose. "Miss Bridget said you've been naughty," the girl told Dowager fondly. Dowager nickered in reply.

Emma stood straighter, assuming the girl was related to Miss Bridget somehow, preparing herself to answer questions about Dowager's pregnancy.

But the girl reached out her hand

for Emma to shake. "I'm Sara," she said, smiling. "All these horses look so happy. You must take wonderful care of them. Thank you for all your hard work."

Surprised, Emma returned Sara's smile. "Thanks," she said. "It's more fun than work, really."

"I can tell," Sara replied. "It must be wonderful to work around horses all day. Aren't they the most amazing creatures?"

"They are," Emma answered. She pointed up at her loft. "I'm here at night, too—that's my room up there."

Sara clapped her hands. "It sounds like a perfect life," she said. "Being with horses all the time . . . even sleeping near them. Your friends must be so jealous. It's like a dream situation."

Emma's smile faltered. She picked up her pitchfork and shuffled straw around in the stall. Biting her lip so she wouldn't burst into tears, Emma wished she saw her life as Sara had described it.

Sara was the first girl her own age she'd spoken to since school let out for the summer, and her happy chatter reminded Emma how lonely she'd been. None of the girls at school were that interested in horses, anyway.

Although Emma loved being with the horses, her life seemed so far away from being a "dream situation" that it was painful to think about. Sara seemed kind, but she didn't know the sad truth. Emma's life would never be perfect again, now that her parents—

A tear fell from Emma's eye and landed in the dirty straw. She glanced over at Sara to see if she had noticed.

Sara wasn't there.

Emma peered around, wondering how Sara had disappeared so quickly. The only person she saw was Brian, hanging up the saddle in the storage area.

It had been great talking with someone who obviously loved horses as much as she did, someone her own age, who seemed cool and kind. Emma hoped that Sara would return soon.

The next morning, when Emma arrived at the stables after breakfast at the house, she was pleased to find Sara in Firelight's stall, brushing the young gray mare. Sara was dressed more casually, in a blue rodeo skirt and beaded shirt, with orange western boots and a white ten-gallon hat. Her outfit looked like an expensive costume, but at least it was a ranch costume and not an English equestrian one.

"Good morning," Emma called. "You're here bright and early."

Sara smiled. "I got the feeling that Firelight needed some extra TLC," she replied. "Not that you don't take great care of her, but she seemed lonely."

Firelight looked thrilled by Sara's grooming. The horse rubbed her muzzle against Sara's arm. "Yeah," Emma said. "She had a special bond with my mom. . . ."

Sara lowered the brush. "Oh, yes," she said softly. "I heard about the accident. No wonder Firelight's sad." Then, sensing Emma's discomfort, she pulled off her hat, revealing braids just like Emma's. "Can you take a break from working today?" Sara asked. "I've got a secret place to show you."

Emma's morning chores had been completed before breakfast. "Sure!" she replied.

Keeping up a steady stream of chatter, Sara led Emma to the far edge of the Day Mare Ranch, past Weeping Willow Lake. Beyond the ranch was an old-growth forest that Emma had barely explored. The forest seemed spooky, but Sara followed a trail without hesitation. She peppered Emma with questions about her favorite things while they walked.

As they chatted, Emma wondered to herself where Sara had come from and what brought her to Miss Bridget's ranch. There was something unusual, something *different* about her, definitely. But Sara's questions came so fast that Emma didn't have a chance to get in any of her own.

"Just up ahead now," Sara said, pointing at a chain-link fence. Whatever had been on the other side was now overgrown with small trees. Emma could make out rundown concrete buildings poking out of the wild shrubs.

Sara ducked through a hole in the fence, and Emma followed. They took a deer path into the overgrown field until they reached a tall concrete structure. Sara cleared brush out of the doorway, and they climbed stairs to an enclosed box perched on top.

The box was clean, except for weeds growing in the corners. It had a wide window, and Emma used it to peer out at the rough field below.

"Do you know what this was?" Sara asked.

Emma shook her head. "An old country club?"

"Nope," Sara replied. "It was a horse racing track, until they built a bigger one. We're in the announcer's box now, where the race callers sat. I come here when I need some alone time."

"Wow," Emma said. Now that Sara had explained, Emma could make out the faded oval track almost hidden by weeds.

"Picture how it used to be," Sara said dreamily. "Can you see the horses? All the trainers and jockeys and the fans? I love imagining how it was."

Emma squinted at the field. For a moment, she could hear the roar of the crowd, the thudding of the horses' hooves as they galloped around the track. She could almost see those horses, their sides heaving with the exhilaration of the race.

"It's amazing," Emma whispered. She smiled at Sara, and Sara grinned back, both delighted to be sharing the secret echoes of those phantom horses.

That afternoon, when they got back to Day Mare Ranch, Emma wanted to share something with Sara, too. "Would you like to meet Mischief?"

"Your Shetland?" Sara replied. "Of course!"

Emma led Sara over to Mischief's stall. The golden coat and white mane and tail of the palomino Shetland looked glossy, since Emma had rubbed him down with a towel that morning. Emma smiled fondly at her pony, her heart softening as it always did when she saw his small, sturdy body.

"Hi, Mischief," Sara said, and the pony made a blow sound through his nose.

Reaching over the gate to ruffle Mischief's mane, Sara noticed his gold hoop earring, and she touched it gently with her finger. "Cute," she said.

"He had that earring when we got

him," Emma explained. "We couldn't remove it without hurting him, but I love it. My father guessed he was rescued from a circus . . . or a pirate!"

Sara and Emma giggled. Then Sara spotted a piece of paper tacked to Mischief's stall. "What's that?"

Emma blushed. "Oh, that's a poem," she answered, torn between wanting to hide it or share it with her new friend. "I wrote it. You can read it, but it's not done yet."

"'With Wings I Can Fly,'" Sara read. "Good title." She read the poem to herself, nodding and smiling.

Emma waited for Sara to finish, feeling embarrassed by how much she wanted Sara to like it.

Sara stood up straight and met Emma's eyes. "It's wonderful," Sara told her. "Really. You should finish it."

"I will," Emma promised, grinning. "As soon as I can think of the perfect ending."

3

That night, Emma had a vivid dream. It had to be a dream, because it was so strange, but it didn't *feel* like a dream.

She rode Mischief along a seashore, the green ocean and yellow sand dazzling in the sunlight. The sky was impossibly blue. Birds swooped overhead, and sandpipers raced alongside Mischief on the shoreline. Emma's hair whipped in the ocean wind.

Emma always loved nature, but now she felt connected to it all, one with the wild world.

In the sea, a fish leaped out of a wave, its scales glinting. It flipped in the air, changing into an incredible half dolphin, half horse creature before diving into the ocean with a mighty splash.

Under Emma, Mischief neighed, and then he changed, too. His compact, strong back grew broader and more muscular. Emma rose higher above the sand as Mischief's legs lengthened. He transformed into a powerful stallion.

Mischief's hooves thundered against the sand.

When Emma woke in her loft bed, she smiled at the dawn sunlight streaming in through her window. The colors of the barn looked brighter and more cheerful than ever before. The heavy sadness that Emma had carried since her parents' accident felt amazingly lighter, as if her spirit were buoyed by a new joy at being alive.

She hopped out of bed, singing to

herself as she got dressed. *"Flying high,"* she sang, making up the lyrics, *"sky high . . . feeling so alive. No more tears to cry . . . when I can fly this high—"*

"Stop that—you're killing me!" her cousin Colm snapped. He was standing near the small desk in front of the stables. "That's the worst song ever. You sound like a croaking bullfrog."

Emma stuck out her tongue, refusing to let him squelch her good mood. "What are you doing out this early, anyway?"

Colm shrugged. "My father needed the inventory book." He held up the ledger. "And here it is, so I can leave you to muck out the stalls. Have a *great* time."

As she worked, Emma kept humming her song and giggling as she imagined every pile of manure looking like Colm's face.

Sara arrived early in the afternoon. This time she was dressed like a country belle, in a flouncy pink dress with a bonnet. She was holding a pink parasol in one hand and carried a package in the other.

Emma laughed at her friend's outfit, delighted by the pretty costume.

"Is it too much?" Sara asked.

"Oh, no," Emma replied. "All you need is a ball to attend, and you're set."

Sara laughed, too. "I dressed up for you," she said. She held out the package, which was wrapped in copper-colored paper and tied with green ribbon. "Happy birthday!"

"How did you know?" Emma asked.

Sara just shrugged. "Go ahead," she urged, "open it. You only turn twelve once."

Emma unwrapped the present. Inside the box was a leather-bound book. Its cover was supple and brown, glowing with gold highlights. Emma ran her finger over the gold embossing on the front, which read THE BALLAD OF EMMA.

In the front corner were the words, *From your friend Sara*, also stamped in gold lettering. A flower design—an orchid—was pressed into the cover.

"Oh, thank you," Emma said. She hugged the book. "I love it. What is a 'ballad'?"

"A ballad is just a fancy name for a song, but I think poems are kind of like songs in a way," Sara answered. "Look inside."

Emma opened the Ballad. The paper was thick and cream-colored, and it tingled under her fingertips.

"Turn the page," Sara suggested. "Now you have an official place to keep all your poems."

Emma flipped the page. She was touched to discover that Sara had written out her unfinished poem "With Wings I Can Fly" in calligraphy. "Now I really will have to think of an amazing ending for it."

"It will come to you," Sara replied.

Emma sighed happily. "This has been the best day," she said. "I had the most incredible dream last night. It was so real, it didn't even feel like a dream."

"You should write it down in the Ballad," Sara suggested. "Dreams like that are a gift . . . they have special power. Writing it down will help you remember."

Emma nodded, and the two girls linked arms as they headed outside to enjoy the summer day together.

That's how Emma and Sara passed all of July—together. They went on picnics beside Weeping Willow Lake, caught fireflies in the fields at dusk, and explored every corner of Day Mare Ranch. They sat by the creek for hours, dangling their feet in the cool water, as they talked. And while it seemed strange that, unlike other kids, Sara didn't ever talk about music, movies, or TV, Emma was amazed by how much they agreed on, especially about food, horses, and treating people respectfully. Although they'd spent only a few weeks together, Emma felt as if she'd known Sara her whole life.

And, of course, all summer long, they hung out with the horses. Sara helped Emma with her chores, and together they made sure that every horse in the stable was groomed and well cared for. They spent afternoons riding through the fields.

Sara knew even more about horses than Emma did. She taught Emma great tricks for handling horses, like putting a dollop of molasses on the bit to get a horse to accept it. Sara also showed Emma the special spot on a horse's crest that they love to have massaged. Emma did that every time she groomed the horses. The best thing Sara taught Emma was a soft song to sing . . . it was wordless, and it worked like a miracle to calm a nervous horse.

One afternoon in early August, Sara and Emma took shelter from a rainstorm in the old announcer's box, where they split a sandwich and munched on apples and carrot sticks.

"Three weeks until school starts," Emma mentioned. "It's turned out to be such a great summer . . . I'm not ready to go back."

"Don't even think about it," Sara replied. "Let's enjoy these days while we have them . . . and let the future take care of itself."

Emma chewed thoughtfully on a carrot. "Well, we'll still be friends when the summer's over," she asked softly, "right?"

Sara rested her head on Emma's shoulder. "We'll be friends for your whole life," she replied. "I promise."

No words had ever made Emma feel happier.

Sara rummaged around in her pack and pulled out a pretty wax candle. "A gift for you," Sara said. "Miss Bridget makes them. Burn it for inspiration when you're writing in your Ballad."

"Thank you," Emma said. "For the candle. For this summer. For everything."

The girls walked back to the ranch through the light drizzle, and when the stables came into sight, Emma announced, "Race you!"

Sara took off running, and Emma, laughing, hurried to catch up. She barely managed to pass Sara through the barn's open door.

What she saw in the stables made her stop short. Walt and Brian were huddled beside Dowager's stall. Uncle Morgan was talking solemnly with Dr. Dwyer, the veterinarian. "What's the matter?" Emma demanded.

Uncle Morgan glanced at her, and then lowered his eyes. "Dowager's foal is coming," he replied. "But something's wrong."

ours later, Dowager was still struggling and gasping for breath as Dr. Dwyer and Walt worked to deliver her foal. The foal was being stubborn about leaving Dowager's womb. The mare whinnied in pain and then groaned as she pushed. Only the foal's front legs had come out so far.

Dr. Dwyer again tried to pull the legs gently toward Dowager's hind hooves, trying to rotate the foal into a better position, but again the foal resisted, and the vet shuffled back. "I can't get hold of the foal's head," he admitted. "The mare is losing blood fast."

"Do what you can, doctor," Uncle Morgan replied, sounding worried.

Sara had disappeared, and Emma watched the delivery with Brian from just outside the stall. Emma winced as Dowager screamed in pain, and she moved closer to the mare's head. Dowager was lying on her side on a pallet of straw.

Emma stroked Dowager's ears. "It will be okay," Emma whispered soothingly to the horse. "It's okay. Your foal will be born safe and strong."

"We need to pull again," Dr. Dwyer announced. "Brian, help me." Brian and the veterinarian each took hold of a leg, using towels to get firmer purchase on the slick limbs. "On the count of three," said Dr. Dwyer. "Firmly but gently." He counted down, and then he and Brian heaved on the legs.

This time, the foal slid forward, his head emerging. Dowager groaned, too exhausted to cry out. Emma kept whispering to her, stroking her head as she shuddered.

Slowly, as Brian and Dr. Dwyer pulled, the foal's shoulders slipped free, followed by the long length of his body, stopping at the hips. Brian and the doctor paused to catch their breath for the final pull. Dowager's eyes rolled up into her head, and her breathing became sharper.

"Again," Dr. Dwyer instructed, and he and Brian pulled the foal once more. His hips sprang out, trailed by his hind legs. The foal was out in the world.

Emma peered over at him. Out of the amnion, the thin gray membrane that had covered him, she could see the color of the foal. He was silvery white, very different from Cookie's rich chestnut. The identity of his sire was still a mystery.

The foal rocked onto his breastbone, whimpering. He tucked his legs under him, trying to stand, but managed only to sit up. He wasn't expected to stand for an hour or so.

Dowager wasn't paying attention to her foal. She kept her head in Emma's lap, her mouth foamy, her eyes still rolled up, her breathing harsh. With the foal stable, Dr. Dwyer turned his attention to Dowager. "She's lost so much blood," the vet said.

"Your foal is here, and safe," Emma whispered to Dowager. "He's beautiful."

"We're losing her," the vet warned.

Emma stroked Dowager's mane, and with a final gasp, the black thoroughbred closed her eyes and died in Emma's lap.

That night, Emma cried herself to sleep. The foal was healthy, but Emma was devastated by Dowager's sacrifice in birthing her colt.

Even though Emma knew she would have to get up in a few hours to help bottle-feed the new foal, she fell into a deep sleep, and she dreamed.

Like the beach dream, this one was so vivid that it felt more like a vision. Hundreds of horses of every breed, size, and color approached the Day Mare Ranch through the misty night.

Emma knew they had come to pay their respects to Dowager, and she found this almost unbearably sad. There was no greater sacrifice than that of a mare giving her life for her foal, and the horses were there to honor her.

The horses surrounded the stables and let out a moan in unison, raising their heads. The mists covering the ranch swept away, and a moonbeam shone down on the still form of Dowager. In the sky was a milky infinity of stars.

The newborn colt, shining silvery in the moonlight, wobbled toward his dam, while the other horses looked on. The colt nuzzled his mother's nose, sniffing.

Emma's heart leaped when Dowager raised her head and met her foal's

muzzle. Joy flooded into Emma, watching the beautiful reunion.

Then the foal broke away from Dowager and hurried to Emma's side. Emma leaned against him as the other horses gathered around Dowager, surrounding her in a tight group.

The horses raised their heads again, and as a single body they began to gallop away. The foal remained beside Emma as the horses stepped into the air, charging into the night.

The herd raced toward the stars, toward ribbons of multicolored light shimmering in the heavens. The waves of color swallowed up the horses, and the aurora borealis faded out, leaving only the twinkling points of stars.

Next to Emma, the foal let out a heartbreaking whinny.

Good-bye.

5

*I*n the morning, Emma was bottle-feeding the foal when Miss Bridget entered the barn. Miss Bridget was a short, plump woman, who looked middle-aged but was probably older. She was wearing a black raincoat and hat. Her face was red and puffy, as if she'd been crying. Emma knew her own face looked just as sad.

Miss Bridget bustled over. "Emma Roland," she said softly, "I've just come from talking to your uncle. We've made arrangements about Dowager's body. We're sending her to the veterinary school, so they can learn from her death."

Emma put the bottle aside and stood up. "I think that's good," she told Miss Bridget. Then she ducked her head. "I'm so sorry about what happened."

"Me too, Emma." Miss Bridget sighed.

"Dowager was a beautiful horse—" Emma began, but then she broke into sobs.

Miss Bridget held out her arms and Emma tumbled into them, and they rocked together in a tight hug. Miss Bridget smelled comforting, like cake and tea.

After a long moment, Miss Bridget let go and wiped her eyes. "All right," she said, "let's see my little guy."

Emma stepped aside so Miss Bridget could take a good look at the foal. Miss Bridget tilted her head as she peered down at the foal. The little foal blinked his eyes. "He's a handsome fellow, isn't he?" Miss Bridget asked. "Look at that silver coat and white mane. I wonder who his sire was."

Emma swallowed nervously. "Miss Bridget," she said, "I hope you know I didn't have anything to do with . . . Dowager getting pregnant. I never let her run free."

"Of course you didn't," Miss Bridget replied. "Oh, I didn't think that for a second. I can tell you understand horses better than that!"

"Thanks," Emma said. "And . . . even though bad things happened to Dowager, I hope . . . I hope you'll keep her colt with us."

Miss Bridget regarded Emma with her watery blue eyes. "You think that's wise? Why should I board him here, after everything that's happened?"

"Because," Emma replied firmly, "I absolutely promise to take better care of him than anyone else. I'll take care of him like he's my own."

Miss Bridget smiled. "Well, of course you will," she said, and once again she opened her arms to envelop Emma in a soft embrace.

Over the next few days, Emma spent all her time with the newborn colt, feeding and bathing him, and making sure he knew he was loved. Emma was so busy that she barely had time to wonder why she hadn't seen Sara since the night Dowager passed away. Since they'd met, Sara had visited every day, and it was strange that she'd been away so long. Emma missed her friend, but she figured that Sara must have her reasons.

One night, Emma was awakened late by the sound of shuffling in the stables below. She sat up and listened intently.

"Be quiet," someone whispered. "Come on."

It was a boy's voice. Emma grabbed a flashlight and climbed down

the ladder as quietly as she could. In the stable aisle, she spotted three shadowy figures in front of Dewdrop's stall. The gate was open, and a boy was leading Dewdrop out of her stall.

"I'll ride this one," the boy hissed. "You get the chestnut across the aisle."

"Stop!" Emma called. "What are you doing to the horses?" She shined the flashlight at the boy, and she recognized her cousin before he raised his hand to block the light. "Colm! You shouldn't be in here."

"Let's go!" one of the other boys shouted, and Colm's two friends bolted out of the stables.

Emma stepped closer to her cousin. "Were you taking them out for night rides?"

"None of your business," Colm shot back. "They're my father's horses now."

Emma ignored that. "It's danger-ous to ride at night. They could stumble on a fence, or step in a gopher hole, or—"

"There was never any problem before you moved in here," Colm snapped. "They were fine."

"You've taken them out before?" Emma demanded. "That's how Dowager—"

"You're crazy," Colm said, looking nervous.

"You can't do this," Emma replied. "It's too dangerous for them. And I'll tell Uncle Morgan unless you stop taking them out at night!"

Colm's face grew red, and his eyes narrowed. "Fine," he spat out, throwing down the reins of Dewdrop's bridle. "You'd better mind your own business and not say anything!"

"These horses are my business," Emma replied firmly, and Colm fled the stables.

After she put Dewdrop back in her stall, Emma climbed up to her loft and tried to go to sleep. But her mind was racing—she was proud of herself for standing up to Colm and furious at her cousin for all his sneaking around. She wished Sara were there to talk to about it.

Emma realized that she could write out her feelings in her Ballad—that was almost as good as talking to Sara directly. She lit Sara's candle and opened her Ballad. Emma wrote about Colm . . . how mean he was to her, how dangerous it was that he took the horses out on night rides . . . and how she suspected that was when Dowager had been out unsupervised—

"You're not going to tell?" Colm asked from behind her. "Swear it!"

Emma jumped in her chair. She hadn't heard him climb up, and now he was standing behind her. "No!" she shot back. "Don't take them out at night again!"

"What are you writing?" Colm asked. He leaned over and read, "'I don't know why Colm is so mean. Maybe it's because he doesn't like himself very much—'" He grabbed the Ballad off the desk. "You can't write that!"

"Give me that back," Emma demanded. "I can write whatever I want!" She tried to snatch the Ballad, but Colm shoved her into her chair.

"'I've often wondered how Dowager got pregnant,'" he continued reading, "'but now I think it's because Colm wasn't careful on these night rides—'" Colm's face turned red again. "That's a lie!" he shouted. "You're writing lies!"

"It's just what I think," Emma protested. "Give me my Ballad back!"

"Oh, your *Ballad*," Colm sneered. "You want it?" He held the book over the candle, letting the flame lap the paper.

"Stop!" Emma cried. She tried to grab the book, but Colm pushed her back again. Emma didn't stop this time, though—she jumped for the book, ducking under his arm. Colm bumped her so that she missed the book. Her hand smacked into the candle, knocking it off the desk. The candle, still burning, rolled across the floor and skidded off the edge of the loft, falling down to the storage area below.

Emma peered down over the railing. The candle had landed in a pile of dry straw. Tongues of flame sprang up in the bale. Smoke wisped up, getting thicker as the flames spread.

"Fire!" Emma shrieked. *"Fire!"*

6

*E*mma whirled around to face Colm, her eyes wild. "We have to get the horses out!"

Colm scooted down the ladder, holding her Ballad. Emma followed.

"Come on!" she shouted, pulling him toward the occupied horse stalls, where the horses were neighing nervously. "Help me!"

Colm stared blankly at the growing fire. It was leaping from bale to bale, blackening the wood walls of the stable.

Emma pushed her cousin. "Help me!"

Shaking off his shock, Colm glanced at her, and then looked over her shoulder at the horses. He blinked, and Emma thought he was going to help rescue the horses. But Colm stepped away from her. He tossed the Ballad into the fire, and then bolted from the stables.

"No!" Emma shrieked, staring at the spot where the book had landed. It was surrounded by flames, deep in the stack of straw. Emma whirled around, searching for a long stick or some tool to knock the Ballad out of the fire.

Behind her, the horses screamed as the fire spread along the walls of the barn.

It would take time to get all the horses out—time Emma couldn't spare to save her Ballad.

With a sob, Emma rushed down the aisle toward the horses. She quickly unlatched all the gates to the stalls and swung the doors open.

Cookie reared up, and then raced out of his stall. He tossed his head and barreled out the barn door to safety.

Seeing Cookie race away, Spaceship bolted out of his stall, following the older stallion.

The other horses, confused by their panic, didn't move. Emma glanced at the newborn foal, who was cowering in the back corner of his stall. "Come on, boy!" Emma shouted, but he backed deeper into the box.

Leaving him for the moment, Emma ran to Dewdrop's stall. As soon as Dewdrop saw Emma, she stepped out of the gate, and Emma pushed her toward the barn exit.

The flames had reached the stable ceiling, burning the beams, racing along the wood. Smoke swirled through the barn, thickening under the eaves. Emma's eyes started stinging and watering, and she coughed from the poisonous fumes. The stables were unbearably hot.

There were still three horses left in the barn—Blinky, Firelight, and the foal—and Emma's pony, Mischief. Emma stood in front of Blinky's stall, begging her to come out. The mare backed up farther, and Emma entered her stall and put her hands along Blinky's head. She pulled gently on her ears, and Blinky lurched forward, following Emma out of the barn.

Firelight had turned around in her stall, shuddering in terror. Emma stepped into her pen, but jumped back when Firelight kicked at her. Emma didn't take it personally—a panicked horse was very dangerous. She took a deep breath, choking on the smoke, and she sang the song Sara had taught her, the wordless tune that calmed horses.

Firelight's ears relaxed, and she turned around. "That's right," Emma whispered. "Good girl, come on." She began singing again, and Firelight exited the stall, following Emma outside.

As Emma turned back to the barn, she gulped—the entire structure was engulfed in flames, with black smoke billowing out. Mischief and the foal were still inside, so Emma ducked low and hurried into the searing heat. She gagged on the smoke and felt painfully light-headed, her vision swimming.

Emma almost fell over from the fumes, but Brian the ranch hand was suddenly there beside her, and he caught her before she fell.

"How many left inside?" Brian demanded.

"Two," Emma said, gasping for breath. "Mischief . . . and . . . the foal."

"Stay outside," Brian ordered. He took a deep breath and ducked down, waddling swiftly into the burning barn.

Emma lost sight of him in the smoke. She coughed harshly, staring into the fire, hoping everyone would be okay.

A few seconds later, Mischief came

trotting out. The pony's eyes were wild and his mane was singed, but otherwise he seemed fine. Emma steered him over to the corral, where the other horses waited. Then she ran back to the stables, getting as close as she could.

For a long time—too long—there was no sign of Brian or the colt. Emma started to cry as the barn doors burst into flames, blocking the exit. How could anyone escape such an inferno?

But then Brian staggered out of the wall of fire with the wriggling foal slung over his shoulders.

Brian lugged the infant horse away from the barn, and he slumped beside Emma, letting the foal slide off his back. Gasping for air, Brian rolled onto his side, and Emma quickly inspected him for any burns. He was covered in soot, and his hair was smoking, but he seemed okay.

"You're out," she sobbed. "You made it."

"They're all out," Brian panted. "They're all safe. I've never been more scared . . . in my whole life." He pushed himself up on all fours and crawled over to the foal.

The foal was breathing irregularly, but whether from shock, smoke inhalation, or some other injury, Emma couldn't tell. Brian pointed out a nasty cut on the little horse's head. Emma rubbed the foal's back, praying he would be all right.

Uncle Morgan, Aunt Cynthia, and Colm ran over from the house, all dressed in pajamas and robes. "The fire department's on their way," Aunt Cynthia told them. "And Dr. Dwyer, too. Is everyone okay?"

"Are all the horses safe?" Uncle Morgan demanded.

Brian nodded. "We got them all out. The foal's injured, but we're not sure how severely yet. His breathing isn't right."

"How did this happen?" Uncle Morgan asked. "Emma, you were in the barn. How did the fire start?"

Emma glanced at Colm. She didn't want to tattle, but she hoped he would take responsibility. This was something nobody could lie about!

"She did it!" Colm cried, pointing at Emma. "She had a candle burning in her room! I told her to put it out!"

Shocked speechless by his lie, Emma gaped at him.

"Is this true?" Uncle Morgan asked. "You had a candle burning in the barn?"

"N-no," Emma stammered. "I mean, yes, I had a candle, but I was careful—"

"What were you thinking?" Uncle Morgan broke in before she could explain. "Don't you know how dangerous open flame is in a barn?"

"I do!" Emma protested. "I didn't—"

"You burned down our barn,"

Aunt Cynthia said, sounding horrified.

"I didn't mean to," Emma sobbed. "I wasn't . . . everything was fine until—"

Uncle Morgan's hands tightened. "There is no possible excuse!" he shouted. "Have you no sense at all? From now on, I forbid you to go near any of these horses!"

"You will stay in the house," Aunt Cynthia added, closing her robe with a white-knuckled fist, "and you will not leave unless we give you permission."

Uncle Morgan nodded. "And you will help your aunt with all the chores until you pay back what you've cost us tonight!" He stomped off to check on the horses in the corral.

Emma looked at Colm, pleading with her tear-filled eyes for him to tell the truth.

But Colm ignored her and ran to join his father.

7

$\mathscr{E}$xhausted and miserable, Emma dropped into sleep in her bedroom in the house.

Another vivid dream descended on her, but this time it was terrifying. She was lost in a forest, fleeing something chasing after her through the trees. The light of the full orange moon seeped through the dense canopy of leaves overhead. Loping, frightening shapes glided through the wood on all sides, snarling.

"It's your fault!" howls taunted her. Emma's blood chilled—she was hearing the vicious voices of wolves. "He'll die!"

Emma stumbled through the underbrush and broke out of the wood into a glade. She ran to a small grassy hill in the center of the clearing and climbed it, while the wolves surrounded her. They snarled as they padded closer.

Slumping on the hill, Emma waited for the wolves.

Then, a glowing white shape leaped gracefully into the glade, landing with heavy hooves beside Emma. She looked up at the most beautiful horse she'd ever seen, a milk-white mare shimmering with an angelic radiance. The mare stood protectively between her and the wolves. The horse snorted a fierce challenge, and the wolves backed off, slinking into the forest.

Emma climbed shakily to her feet, bathed in the light cast by the white horse. A strong, clear image flashed in Emma's mind—herself atop the mare in the clearing. The horse blinked, and Emma, astounded, realized that the

image had been sent *from* the mare. Emma trembled as the horse lowered her body so Emma could mount.

"Thank you," Emma whispered, as she climbed onto the mare.

All her fear was wiped away as the mare ran through the forest. Her speed was fantastic, and Emma felt filled with freedom, knowing everything would turn out better than she had dared hope—

"Get up," Aunt Cynthia said, waking Emma by pulling back her blanket. "You've got nothing but work today."

Aunt Cynthia gave her a list of chores: cleaning the oven, polishing the hardwood floors, vacuuming the rooms, dusting all the furniture in the living room and parlor, and doing everyone's laundry. Emma threw herself into the work—it was better to be busy with mindless tasks rather than think about how terrible her life had become.

Around lunchtime, Emma had finished vacuuming the ground floor and moved to the carpeted front stairs when the vacuum bag filled up. She headed toward the kitchen to get a replacement bag.

As she walked down the hall, she could hear Aunt Cynthia talking to Uncle Morgan. "What are we going to do with that girl?" Uncle Morgan asked, and Emma froze outside the kitchen door, listening. "You know we promised we'd look after her, and she is family, but we can't just let her mope around the house forever."

"She's a dark cloud of mope," Aunt Cynthia agreed.

"I realize the fire was an accident," Uncle Morgan continued, "but she should've known better. We're barely holding on to the ranch. With the stable gone—"

Aunt Cynthia snorted. "I'm not sure it *was* an accident," she said. "Colm told me she started the fire on purpose. His take is that Emma can't stand us running the ranch instead of her parents, and she's lashing out."

Emma covered her mouth to stifle her gasp and leaned closer to hear Uncle Morgan's reply. "I can't trust her around the horses," he said, "and we can't lock her in the house. School starts soon, but what is she going to do in the afternoons? All she ever did was work in the barn. I don't see an end to her misery."

"Or ours," Aunt Cynthia added. "Unless . . ."

Emma closed her eyes, afraid to hear Aunt Cynthia's next words.

"What if she went to school . . . elsewhere?" Aunt Cynthia suggested. "I looked up a boarding school on the Internet."

Emma hurried away from the kitchen door. Boarding school! She couldn't leave the ranch! It was her last link to her parents. And she wouldn't see Mischief or any of the horses anymore, and she would lose touch with Sara.

Emma had promised Miss Bridget that she would take care of the new colt, and how could she do that from a boarding school?

Emma stopped near the front door, catching her breath. Not that she'd done a good job taking care of the foal. He'd almost died in the fire, and she'd heard that he was still very sick for reasons Dr. Dwyer didn't fully understand—perhaps because of smoke inhalation or the nasty cut he'd gotten on his head.

Clenching her hands, Emma realized that she had to check on the colt, even if it was forbidden. If he should die—

That was another terrible thought to avoid.

Emma slipped out the front door and hurried around the house, heading toward the pasture, where a shelter had been set up for the horses.

As she got closer, she spotted an unfamiliar trailer attached to a pickup truck. Emma ducked behind a tree.

Colm came around from behind the trailer to open its rear gate. Then Brian appeared, leading Mischief by a tether. He led Emma's pony up to the ramp.

Emma bolted toward the trailer. "Where are you taking him?"

Smirking, Colm stepped between Emma and Mischief. "He's been sold."

"You can't sell him!" Emma protested. "He's not yours to sell—he's mine!"

"You should've thought about that before you burned down the barn," Colm replied. "We've got no place to keep him, and we've got to support the horses."

"*You* burned the barn," Emma shot back. "Not me!"

"That's crazy," Colm said calmly. "It wasn't my candle."

Emma looked at Brian, who had his head lowered. "Brian, please,"

Emma said softly. "Don't let them take my Mischief."

Brian raised his kind face, and Emma started to cry when she saw that his blue eyes were red and watery. "I'm truly sorry," Brian said. "There's . . . there's nothing I can do."

A sob racked Emma's chest, and she sprinted toward the house, wiping her tears as she ran.

When she reached the back porch, Emma threw herself on a bench under the open kitchen window and wept against her arm.

Everything she loved had been taken away. She sobbed for the loss of her parents, for Dowager's sad death, for Sara who had disappeared, for her banishment from working with the horses, for the accident that burned the barn, for the sick foal, and now for poor Mischief, who hadn't done anything except be the sweetest pony in the world.

Emma's heartbreak was so overwhelming that she couldn't imagine how anything could be good again.

That's when Dr. Dwyer and Uncle Morgan came out of the house on the other side of the porch. They didn't notice Emma, and she stifled a sniffle, listening to their conversation. Maybe Dr. Dwyer had news about the foal. . . .

"It's not good," Dr. Dwyer said. "If the colt doesn't improve soon, well, I'm sorry to say, it would be kinder to put him down."

Uncle Morgan shook his head. "First Dowager, and now this," he muttered darkly. "Losing our only boarder . . . how can we explain that to Bridget? Our reputation will never recover."

Emma wrapped her arms around herself, shuddering. It seemed so heartless of Uncle Morgan to worry about the ranch's reputation when the foal's life was in danger.

A noise above her made Emma look up. Aunt Cynthia peered out the window, listening to her husband and the veterinarian. When Aunt Cynthia spotted Emma, her eyes narrowed.

"You hear that, Emma?" Aunt Cynthia snapped. "We're ruined. And you know whose fault that is, don't you?"

Emma shut her eyes.

"Yours," Aunt Cynthia said, bursting into tears herself.

Emma bolted off the bench and jumped off the low porch. She sprinted across the lawn. She didn't know where she was running to, but she knew she had to get far away from all the guilt and misery that hung over the house like a thunderstorm.

Losing steam at the edge of the ranch's farthest field, Emma slowed to a dawdle, trudging across the grass. She stepped grimly, trying to keep her mind blank.

She stumbled down a path surrounded by shrubbery. Brambles pulled at her sleeves, but she barely noticed.

She wandered until mists rose around her, steaming off Weeping Willow Lake. She focused on the sounds of crickets chirping and dragonflies buzzing, shutting out the terrible voices in her head.

At the lake's edge, Emma sat on a fallen log, staring blankly at the misty water. The fog thickened around her, moisture collecting on her face and on the leaves of the willows, dripping slowly back into the lake. She was crying again, her tears mixing with the damp air.

Emma felt so lost that the first soft neigh nearby barely registered.

The whisper of a neigh came again, low and insistent, and Emma turned her head to look.

A few steps away on the shore, a white horse emerged from the mist.

It was the magnificent mare from her dream. Emma slumped her shoulders, staring at the horse's brilliant white coat, her gorgeous mane, her head that looked carved out of marble. She met the mare's liquid eyes, and a warm sense of ease washed over her.

The horse neighed softly again and nodded her head. An image of Emma approaching the mare blinked in Emma's brain, and she stood and walked toward the horse. As she neared, she stretched out her hand, and the mare met it with her nose, warming it with her breath.

A calm settled over Emma. Peace soothed her broken heart, and her limbs felt leaden with weariness. She weaved on her feet, suddenly exhausted.

Emma backed up, and let herself slump to the grassy shore, giving in to her drowsiness.

She curled up beside the fallen log and slept.

8

*S*ometime later, Emma stirred, hearing faint voices. She opened her eyes and saw that dusk had fallen. The mare glowed white nearby, watching over her. A girl stood by the mare, stroking the horse's nose tenderly. The girl wore a hood and silvery robes that shone with a soft radiance.

Emma sat up groggily. "Am I dreaming?" The girl lowered her hood. It was Sara, but her face seemed so perfect that Emma wasn't sure she recognized her friend.

"You're dreaming," Sara replied with a smile, "and you're not dreaming. We're together between the worlds."

Emma nodded as though that made sense.

"I see you've met my best friend," Sara said. "This is Bella." Bella bowed in greeting.

"You should feel honored," Sara continued, sounding much more solemn than the giggly girl Emma had known. "Bella likes you as much as I do, and she's very choosy about her friends."

"She's lovely," Emma whispered. "I love her already." She swallowed, tears threatening to overspill her eyes again. "Sara, where were you?" Emma asked. "Everything became so horrible, and I was all alone. I thought you were my friend—"

"I am your friend," Sara replied firmly, "and I'm more than your friend. I've been watching over you, the same way I've watched over you since you were born. I've been protecting you, watching you grow from a little girl into a young woman, blossoming like this orchid." Sara reached out her hand toward a stem growing beside the tree trunk.

Emma felt a rush of power pass through her, and her eyes widened as the bare stem thickened and stretched and developed a series of tender buds, which opened into purple and white blooms. The orchid flowers matched the engravings that had been on the cover of *The Ballad of Emma*.

"Now I know this is a dream," Emma murmured.

"I remember when you told me your dreams," Sara replied. "They are *visions*, a peek at a place that's very real. I know it sounds strange, but you were seeing the home of your ancestors. You were born here on Earth, but you are the last descendant of a woman from our world, a mighty Valkyrie named Sigga."

"A *Valkyrie*?" Emma asked. "Are

you making this up?"

"It's all true," Sara answered. "Valkyries are powerful, brilliant women. They ride magic steeds and roam the worlds picking heroes, granting inspiration and courage. They live in a place called North of North, beyond the aurora borealis. Sigga was our greatest Valkyrie. Her blood flows in your veins."

Emma tried to make sense of all this. Sara seemed different now, filled with a power that frightened Emma. "I don't understand you," Emma whispered.

"I'm sorry," Sara said with a smile, "but I've got so much to tell you, and there isn't enough time to fully explain. You are the first female born in the Roland line in a millennium, since Sigga fell in love with a mortal and was cast out by the Alfather, the creator of all things in North of North. Sigga's family was cursed to bear only sons, and boys can't become Valkyries. But now we've got *you*. It's time to claim your heritage."

"My heritage?" Emma asked, bewildered. "These dreams are getting crazier. When I wake up, Sara, I'll tell you all about this and we'll laugh, okay?"

Sara didn't smile. "I know it sounds unbelievable, but you're awake—more awake now than ever. You're a Valkyrie of the House of Sigga, the first in an age, and we don't have any time to lose."

Emma shook her head, trying to wake up. She pinched herself on the arm, but it only hurt. Sara still stood in front of her, staring solemnly.

"In time you'll understand," Sara said. "You are a Valkyrie. You'll become the leader of the House of Sigga, with the power to heal—"

"Heal?" Emma interrupted. "You mean, I'll be able to heal the sick colt . . . ?"

"Of course, but only after you claim your birthright and accept the power of the Valkyrie world."

"How . . . how do I do that? The foal is very weak, and the vet said—"

"You must be strong, Emma," Sara broke in. "You've got to realize the power within you. You'll need to prove to the Valkyries that you're a daughter in the line of Sigga Rolanddotter. Only then will they let you join them."

"To help the foal," Emma swore, "I'll do anything."

Sara nodded. "Hestheim, the Valkyrie home, is in North of North. It floats on a cloud above the Auroborus, so you'll need to fly, of course. You'll love flying on horseback, you'll see. I'll send Sigga's stallion, Valkrist, to help you."

Bella whinnied at the sound of Valkrist's name.

"Nobody has ridden Valkrist since Sigga," Sara continued. "Trust in him, and believe in yourself."

"I will," Emma promised. "Thank you, Sara."

"Good luck, Emma Roland," Sara said. "I have faith in you."

Sara swung herself onto Bella's back. She waved at Emma once, and then Bella pivoted and swiftly carried Sara away from Weeping Willow Lake, until they vanished into the mist.

9

s soon as Sara and Bella vanished, the mists around the lake swirled, dissipating into the night. A wash of twinkling stars became visible, overlaid with ribbons of twisting light— the aurora borealis. Staring at those colors shifting in the sky, Emma's eyes widened when a fiery glow broke free of the aurora. The gold light streaked toward Emma like a shooting star.

The golden glow zoomed overhead, and then circled back toward the clearing. Emma gasped when she saw

that the glow was a flying silvery horse
. . . a horse with wings the color of molten gold!

The stallion swooped lower, his
enormous wingspan trailing a stream
of light that gushed out in shimmering
whorls of energy. Tucking his wings, the
horse landed in front of Emma with a
solid thump.

The horse neighed, and Emma
saw that he resembled the breed Akhal-
Teke, but with a more muscular chest.
Like his wings, the horse's mane and tail
rippled like molten gold, and his bright
eyes swirled with golden fire. His coat
was silvery-white, like the surface of a
marble statue. The stallion had a tattoo
of a purple orchid on his hip. He neighed
again, tossing his head at Emma, his
wings shimmering.

"Valkrist?" Emma whispered, wondering again if she were dreaming.

Valkrist whinnied. He kneeled
in front of Emma, opening his wings

slightly to give her space to mount. Like when Emma had met Bella in her dream, Valkrist sent a clear invitation into Emma's mind, an image of her riding toward the stars. Moving in a daze, Emma climbed onto Valkrist and dug her fingers into his soft mane.

Valkrist stood and peered back to make sure Emma was holding on securely. When she nodded, Valkrist spread his wings and broke into a run toward the lake.

Before they hit the water, Valkrist flapped his wings twice, and then they were airborne. His hooves splashed trails into the surface of the lake. He circled upward, and then cleared the trees, soaring into the night.

Emma held on tightly with her hands and legs. She was astounded by the thrilling speed of their rise, awed by the power of the muscular winged stallion beneath her. She had to remind herself to breathe.

In moments, they had streaked up so high that the surface of the Earth was left far below. Emma faced upward as they rushed toward the twisting lights of the aurora borealis.

The aurora wasn't merely light—it was energy. It surrounded Emma and prickled her skin as they entered the flickering ribbons of color. The flashing aurora grew brighter around her until she was nearly blinded by the dazzling lights. Emma ducked her head against Valkrist's mane, breathing in his scent, which was reassuringly like the familiar smell of every horse she'd ever known.

Valkrist beat his golden wings more strongly, and with a last great flash, they passed through the light. Darkness settled around them.

Emma raised her head. The stars above were in different positions from where she remembered, with strange cosmic formations and oddly colored streaks of galaxies. Looming in space was an enormous planet, a massive gas giant circled by rings.

Valkrist banked, heading toward a thick blanket of dark storm clouds below. As they entered the storm, lightning streaked nearby. An explosion of thunder made Emma want to cover her ears. But she didn't let go of Valkrist's mane. She felt surprisingly safe atop the stallion.

Valkrist plunged out of the storm cloud into a clear sky. The sky was made up of the pastel colors of dawn. As they raced past the clouds, Emma spotted buildings and stretches of forest or farmland, but Valkrist didn't get close enough to see clearly.

Then a fortress loomed up, with tall silvery-gray towers jutting out of a thick cloud bank. As they neared it, Emma saw that the fortress was massive, with curved walls and towering spires, like a fountain frozen into spikes of stone.

Valkrist dived toward the fortress

and barreled through the open front gate. He slowed in the arched hallway inside, his feet clomping on the marble floor as he landed. Valkrist trotted forward, carrying Emma into a huge circular room with an enormous vaulted ceiling.

The first thing Emma noticed in the room was a series of niches inset along the curved wall. Each niche had a symbol carved into the wall above it, and a name inscribed below. Emma read the names Valda, Haldis, Thessa, Runa, Rianna . . . and the last one, Sigga. That was the name Sara had said, the name of her ancestor! It saddened Emma to see that Sigga's alcove was dusty with neglect.

Valkrist took Emma to the center of the circular room, where five imposing women dressed in armor were waiting. Valkrist sent an image of Emma talking to these warrior women—they were obviously the Valkyries Sara told her about. When the stallion stopped in front of the Valkyries, Emma dismounted.

The biggest of the Valkyries stepped forward. She was a tall warrior dressed in black armor, and she had bright gold-braided hair. "What do you think you're doing here?" she demanded.

Emma took a deep breath. "Um, hi. Hello. My name . . . I am Emma Roland. I . . . I am . . . a daughter in the line of Sigga."

The Valkyries glanced at one another, and then they laughed harshly.

"The line of Sigga, you say?" asked a round-faced Valkyrie with a coil of brown hair. "The line of Sigga has no daughters. If you believe this to be true, show us your Ballad!"

"My Ballad?" Emma replied. She lowered her head. "It was . . . burned in a fire, by accident. I'm really sorry."

A tall, willowy, white-haired Valkyrie laughed again. "Now we know you're lying," she said. "Valkyrie Ballads are made by Sara, goddess of horses. They do not burn and cannot be destroyed."

"But—" Emma began.

She was interrupted by a short, slim Valkyrie with long black hair, who raised her hands for silence. The Valkyrie was wearing a black tunic that left her pale arms exposed. Emma squinted at her—she seemed to radiate darkness. The dark Valkyrie clapped her hands sharply, and a white light exploded out from her, dazzling Emma's eyes with searing brightness.

When Emma's vision cleared, the Valkyries were gone, and she was standing on the grassy shore of Weeping Willow Lake. She blinked her sore eyes, peering around for Valkrist, but the winged horse was nowhere to be seen. The Valkyries had sent her back.

Emma's heart sank. She'd failed to convince the Valkyries. How could she save the foal now? She had to win over the Valkyries somehow . . . but how was that possible without her Ballad?

Weary from her journey and miserable over her failure, Emma slumped down on a bed of soft moss as the sun rose.

10

"*E*mma?" asked a sweet voice.

Emma raised her head, hoping to see Sara entering the glade. She had so many questions for her—starting with asking about the phrase *goddess of horses.*

But it wasn't Sara.

Miss Bridget, wearing a black hat, yellow raincoat, and black boots, hurried toward Emma, her face concerned. "Emma, dear," Miss Bridget asked, "were you out here all night?"

"I don't know where I've been,"

Emma replied.

"I know where you're going," Miss Bridget said. "You're coming home with me." She pulled Emma up from the moss patch with a strong grip. Still feeling weary, Emma didn't protest when Miss Bridget brushed her clean of twigs and dirt. Then Miss Bridget took Emma's hand and led her away from Weeping Willow Lake.

Miss Bridget took a winding route through the wood, the underbrush seeming to open up in front of her.

They wound around a hill, and Emma saw a cute cottage shaded by old hickory trees. Orchids twined up the trees and surrounded the cottage with beautiful blossoms in every shade of purple.

Miss Bridget led Emma up a path of white stones and inside the cozy cottage, which was warm and dry thanks to a cheery fire in the hearth. Emma sat in the little parlor on a soft loveseat.

"You have a nice rest there," Miss

Bridget said, "and I'll bring you some tea and buttered toast."

Emma looked around the parlor, taking in the watercolors of purple orchids on the walls, the statues of horses on the mantle, and the landscape drawings of places that didn't look quite real.

Emma sat up, startled, when a pair of mice popped up on an end table and stared at Emma with bright, beady eyes. The mice had multiple long tails braided with purple ribbons.

"What are those?" Emma asked, when Miss Bridget came back carrying a tray.

Miss Bridget glanced over and smiled. "Oh, just a couple of tassel mice, dear," she replied. "Lovely little darlings, aren't they?"

Emma nodded, and the tassel mice chattered happily and dived behind the table.

Miss Bridget joined Emma on

the loveseat. She poured tea and placed a warm cup in Emma's hands. "Now, dear," Miss Bridget said, "I expect you've seen some wonderful things recently. Why don't you tell me all about it?"

"I don't know where to begin."

"At the beginning," Miss Bridget replied kindly.

"It will sound . . . crazy," Emma warned.

Miss Bridget patted Emma's knee. "I'm sure it won't. Have a piece of toast, dear."

Emma took some toast and told Miss Bridget everything. She started with Sara and explained the visions she'd been having. Miss Bridget nodded with understanding, so Emma told her about Bella and the unbelievable things Sara had told her by Weeping Willow Lake. Then Emma explained as best she could about her amazing trip on Valkrist to the fortress of the Valkyries, and how they hadn't believed her and sent her home.

"So now I have to prove I'm from the line of Sigga somehow," Emma finished up, "but they won't believe me without the Ballad. I don't know what to do." She peered over at Miss Bridget's cheerful face. "I told you it was a strange story."

"Not at all," Miss Bridget said. "Have some more toast, dear." When Emma was munching away on a second slice, Miss Bridget continued. "I have a small confession to make," she admitted. "Everything Sara told you was true. I was once your great-great-great-grandmother Sigga's handmaid. There are more 'greats' in there, I think. I was gifted with a very long life indeed. Like Sara, I've watched over your family for hundreds of years."

Emma stopped chewing on her toast. "You . . . you don't *look* that old."

Miss Bridget laughed. "I don't feel that old," she replied. "Life is a pleasure when you fill it with love and devotion." She stood up abruptly, strode over to a cabinet, and pulled out an object wrapped in white cloth. "Here," Miss Bridget said. "It's Sigga's Ballad. All the Valkyries documented their travels and important deeds in journals just like this. You'll need Sigga's Ballad to prove who you are."

Emma unwrapped the package . . . and found a Ballad that almost matched the one she had lost in the fire. The only difference was a golden lock attached to a clasp that held the book closed. Emma fumbled with the lock, but it wouldn't open.

"You'll need the key," Miss Bridget explained. "Only you can find it."

Emma frowned at the lock. "I don't know where to look. It could be anyplace."

"Oh, no," Miss Bridget replied. "You will find the answer in the place where answers have always come to you."

"And where's that?" Emma asked.

Miss Bridget smiled. "In your dreams, of course," she answered. Miss Bridget faced Emma. "Now lie back," she instructed, "and relax."

Emma slumped into the loveseat as Miss Bridget began to recite a poem in her sweet voice:

"O, sing with me, sisters, here in our hall,
In North of North beyond Bella's Lights!
Sing once more the history of heroes,
And tell the story of our birthright.

We are the Valkyries, the sisters of Sigga,
Brave sky-riders on magical steeds.
We soar on the winds of a thousand worlds
In search of the heroes our destiny needs.

All great stories of glorious adventure
Begin with Valkyries, who must inspire
Our heroes to find the wisdom and courage
Their noble quests will soon require.

And when our heroes return victorious,

Their tales of adventure we carefully write

On gold-edged pages in our Ballads,

Memories of valor immortal and bright.

So sing, my sisters, of friendship and honor.

Sing of our duty, done wisely and well.

Sing a salute to the next rising hero,

Whose story we all are most eager to tell."

Lulled by the sound of the poem, the warmth of the fire, and the gentle tea, Emma's eyes closed. When she blinked them open again, she was in the great hall of the Valkyries, watching as the warrior women solemnly proceeded toward the alcoves.

One by one, the Valkyries stepped forward. The willowy, white-haired one placed a long white feather in the alcove that read VALDA under it. The feather matched the symbol carved into the stone above.

Next was the short, plump Valkyrie, who placed a golden sphere into the alcove marked HALDIS. Haldis was followed by the giant blond Valkyrie, who put a jeweled dagger into the RIANNA niche. The smallest Valkyrie stepped forward after Rianna, placing pine branches into the THESSA alcove. Last, the pale, dark-haired warrior approached her niche, adding a burning candle into the alcove marked RUNA. All their offerings matched the runes carved above the recessed niches.

Emma peered closely at the alcove marked SIGGA.

The symbol above the niche was a small, beautifully carved orchid.

Emma woke up with a start on Miss Bridget's loveseat. "I know what to do!"

"Yes, dear," Miss Bridget replied with a smile. "I'm sure you do."

Emma returned Sigga's handmaid's smile. "Miss Bridget," she asked, "would it be okay if I took some of your orchids?"

11

*M*iss Bridget led Emma back to Weeping Willow Lake. Emma was carrying a vase of purple orchid blossoms in her arms.

"Call for him, dear," Miss Bridget suggested.

Emma nodded. "Valkrist!" she called out. "Please, I need you!"

Staring into the overcast sky, Emma couldn't make out the aurora borealis behind the gray clouds. She just had to have faith that it was there, shimmering in space.

Sure enough, a golden shape broke through the clouds and swooped overhead, beating his wings that streamed out ripples of golden light.

"He was always such a fancy guy," Miss Bridget commented fondly.

"He's gorgeous," Emma breathed, as Valkrist soared closer and landed in front of them.

Valkrist neighed in greeting and kneeled down before Emma so she could climb aboard.

Emma held on to his glowing mane with one hand and tucked the vase of orchids securely into her other arm as Valkrist spread his wings and took off. Holding on, Emma couldn't return Miss Bridget's wave as Valkrist carried her up into the clouds.

Once again, the journey through the aurora borealis to the realm of North of North was breathtaking. Even as concerned as she was with her plan working, Emma was astounded by riding Valkrist through the aurora and beyond, into a world floating on clouds.

Valkrist took Emma directly into the Valkyries' fortress, and Emma dismounted in the massive vaulted chamber.

"She dares to return!" Valda, the willowy, white-haired Valkyrie, cried.

Along with Valda, Haldis, the short, stocky Valkyrie, hurried toward Emma, but Rianna, the giant golden-haired warrior, blocked their path.

"Let us see what she will do," Rianna said.

Emma strode toward the alcoves, the thumping of her boots sounding incredibly loud. She passed the glaring Valkyries and stepped up to the niche marked SIGGA.

Taking a deep breath, Emma placed her vase of orchids in the dusty alcove.

For a long, disappointing moment, nothing happened.

"Please," Emma whispered. "I brought you orchids. I am a daughter in the line of Sigga. I believe. I *believe.*"

Almost too faint to see, a dim glow shimmered in the alcove.

"Yes," Emma said, hope blazing up within her. "I am here."

The glow grew stronger behind the orchids, a deep purple light that radiated outward in lavender rays. Emma took a step backward as the light became brighter, and then she shielded her eyes against an explosion of dazzling brilliance.

The light faded, leaving behind wriggling sparks that spiraled out from the alcove like a swarm of fireflies.

The vase of orchids was gone.

In its place was a metal shield emblazoned with an amethyst orchid in its center.

"Who gave you the right to call on the power of Sigga's house?" Runa, the pale, dark-haired Valkyrie, demanded.

Instead of answering, Emma stepped forward and lifted the shield out

of the alcove. The shield was thick and heavy—more than a mere decoration, it was meant for battle.

Emma raised the shield. "I am a daughter in the line of Sigga!" she called. "Here is the proof!"

Thessa, the short, mousy, brown-haired warrior, strode over to Emma and took the shield from her. "We are impressed," she said. "Sigga's alcove has not responded to any offering in a millennium." Thessa glanced back at the other Valkyries, who all nodded solemnly. "Please wait out in the hall with Valkrist while we discuss your claim."

Emma nodded, and then decided that something more formal was due such impressive warrior women, so she bowed, almost losing her balance. Then Emma led Valkrist out into the hall with its arched ceiling. She glanced back as a wooden door swung closed, and she caught a glimpse of the Valkyries gathering together with serious expressions on their faces.

It was a long wait. Emma stroked Valkrist while she waited, and was amused that the stallion let her know what spots he wanted rubbed or scratched by sending more wordless images into her mind.

Finally, the door swung open again, and Emma and Valkrist walked back into the vaulted chamber. The Valkyries stood in a line facing Emma, with Rianna holding the shield.

"We have come to a decision," Rianna announced.

Emma held her breath.

"You are still too young," Rianna said. "Return when you have come into your own more completely."

Emma exhaled in disappointment.

"Do not despair, young one," Thessa said reassuringly. "You will soon be among us. Meanwhile, take Sigga's shield as a sign of your heritage. We shall await your return, little sister."

Realizing that they believed her, Emma grinned. She bowed deeply to the Valkyries and took the shield from Rianna.

The Valkyries all returned Emma's bow.

Valkrist brought Emma back to Earth as fast as he could fly, and dropped her off beside Weeping Willow Lake. As soon as Emma was clear, Valkrist reared up majestically and whinnied. He zoomed away, his wings trailing golden light, and Emma waved to him until he disappeared into the clouds.

Emma carried the shield toward Miss Bridget's cottage, amazed at how the forest opened up a path in front of her that led her to the fields of flowers.

When Emma reached the cottage, Miss Bridget threw open the front door, clapping her hands in delight. "You've done it!" Miss Bridget cheered. "Congratulations, Emma! That's wonderful."

"Thank you," Emma replied,

entering the cottage.

As Emma settled on the loveseat, Miss Bridget took out Sigga's Ballad again and placed it on the low table. "If you can find a way to open this book," Miss Bridget explained, "you may find the answers you seek."

Emma nodded and peered closely at the orchid design on the Ballad's lock. Then she examined the shield. Both objects had the same purple orchid on them.

Pulling the shield closer, Emma rubbed her fingers along the jeweled amethyst orchid on its center. It was raised slightly. Emma tugged at the orchid with her fingertips and smiled when it shifted.

After more prodding, a petal of the orchid sprang loose. Emma held it up—the petal had a small stem attached. It would fit into the Ballad's lock perfectly!

With trembling hands, Emma unlocked the clasp on Sigga's Ballad.

The pages were filled with ornate

handwriting, scrawled in a language Emma could barely understand. It would take a long time to figure out all her ancestor's words.

Then a loose letter slipped free of the pages and landed in Emma's lap.

Emma picked up the letter. On the front was written *To Emma*. A chill tingled down Emma's spine.

The back of the letter was closed with a wax seal imprinted with an orchid. Emma broke the seal and unfolded the letter, her hands shaking.

On the paper, in Sigga's handwriting, was written four lines of a poem.

Emma scanned the words and burst into tears. Those four lines made up the final stanza of her own poem, "With Wings I Can Fly."

She had found the perfect ending.

"*L*eave those here," Miss Bridget said, waving her hand at the shield and Sigga's Ballad. "I'll take good care of them for you."

Emma stood in Miss Bridget's parlor, chewing her lip. She had confronted powerful Valkyries, but she was feeling nervous about seeing her aunt and uncle again. "Can't I stay here for awhile?"

"You could," Miss Bridget replied. "But don't you want to put the pieces of your poem together?"

"If the copy in Mischief's stall

survived," Emma said glumly. "I have Sigga's stanza in my pocket. But—"

"But nothing," Miss Bridget said. "You have to go home eventually. I'm sure your family wonders where you are."

"So they can punish me more," Emma said. "Or send me to boarding school."

"Huh," Miss Bridget said, shooing Emma toward the door. "You don't sound like a Valkyrie-to-be, daughter in the line of Sigga. Don't you at least want to see how our foal is doing?"

Emma nodded. Miss Bridget held the door open, and Emma trudged outside. "I can come back and visit, right?"

"Of course," Miss Bridget answered. "Anytime. And no matter what happens, I will always be nearby."

Emma kissed Miss Bridget on the cheek. Then she squared her shoulders and strode through the flowers, heading back to face whatever she might find at Day Mare Ranch.

Emma knew her Ballad had been destroyed, but maybe the original poem in the stall hadn't burned. She peeked into the charred shell of the stables. All the interior structures had been removed.

A blue tarp had been hung like a tent near the corral, and Emma could see that surviving tools and tack had been stacked under it, along with lumber that hadn't burned. At one end of the pasture, tarps had been set up as stalls for the horses. Emma hurried over to the tarp covering the salvage.

Emma examined the stacks of lumber. Maybe her poem was still tacked to one of the planks. She lifted a few boards, but didn't see any sign of her poem.

"Emma!" Uncle Morgan's voice called out.

Flinching, Emma stood up and turned around. Uncle Morgan was standing behind her, smiling.

"Oh, it's so good to see you're okay," Uncle Morgan said. "When you didn't come home, your aunt was so worried—"

"She was?" Emma asked.

"Of course she was!" Uncle Morgan replied. "I know awful things were said—we were all emotional after the fire. But we're your family."

Emma ducked her head. "I was with Miss Bridget," she explained. "I'm sorry I ran away."

"I'm just glad you're safe," Uncle Morgan said. "Now, what were you doing over here? Looking for this?"

Uncle Morgan held out her Ballad.

Emma's mouth dropped open. "But I saw it burn," she whispered, taking the book. It wasn't damaged at all.

Uncle Morgan cleared his throat. "I hope you don't mind, but I read it," he said. "And . . . I want to apologize to you. What you wrote about Colm . . . he confessed when I asked him about the night rides. He also admitted that he'd been teasing you with the candle when it got knocked over. I'm sorry we didn't believe you."

Emma hugged the Ballad to her chest. "So you're not mad at me?" she asked. "No boarding school?"

"No, no, this ranch is your home," Uncle Morgan replied. "In fact, I would be honored if you could forgive me enough to start helping out with the horses again."

Emma nodded, allowing herself to smile. "I would love to," she said. "Can I ask . . . what about Mischief?"

"Well, the pony is sold," Uncle Morgan said, sighing. "Honestly, it's best for him to be at another ranch." Seeing the pleading look in Emma's eyes, her uncle softened. "Once we get back on our feet, we'll see about buying him back. Okay? I miss the little guy, too."

Uncle Morgan put his arm around Emma's shoulders. As they stepped out from under the tarp, they saw Colm lounging against the pipe fence of the corral.

"Hold on a moment," Uncle Morgan told Emma. He ducked back under the tarp and came out with a shovel. "Colm," he called out, "get over here!"

Colm dawdled over, avoiding meeting Emma's eyes. "What?"

Uncle Morgan handed Colm the shovel. "Your new job is to clean out the makeshift stalls every morning. Starting now."

Colm stared at the shovel in his hands in shock. "But, *Dad*—"

"That manure won't wait," Uncle Morgan replied, crossing his arms. "It's going to take months for you to work off the price of a new barn!"

His face red, Colm strode off toward the tarp stalls, grumbling. When he was gone, Emma put her hand on Uncle Morgan's arm. "The foal," she asked. "How is he?"

Uncle Morgan heaved a deep breath. "Not great news there, I'm afraid," he admitted. "Dr. Dwyer says that if the colt doesn't get better by tomorrow . . . well, it would be kinder to put him down." He patted Emma's hand. "Let's go see him now, okay?"

Emma nodded, and Uncle Morgan led her over to the tarp where the foal was sheltered. The colt was lying on a bed of clean straw, his chest heaving with harsh breathing. Emma kneeled down and checked out his injury. The cut on his head was swollen and dark with infection. Tears heated Emma's eyes as she stroked the foal's nose.

"Is it okay . . . ," Emma began. "Can I be alone with him for a while?"

"Okay," Uncle Morgan answered. "You call for me if you need anything."

"Thank you," Emma whispered.

As soon as Uncle Morgan was gone, Emma sat beside the foal and rubbed his back. "I'm going to find a way to make you better," she promised.

Emma opened her Ballad. On the front page were the first nine stanzas of her poem, written out in Sara's lovely handwriting. Emma pulled Sigga's letter out of her pocket and smoothed it open. Then she grabbed the pen off the veterinarian's chart hanging on a pole.

In her best script, Emma copied the last stanza of the poem from the letter into the Ballad. Her hand tingled as she wrote, and the air under the tarp seemed to crackle with energy. The whole ranch felt as though it were holding its breath.

When Emma wrote the final word, the letters of the poem glowed briefly. She knew she had connected this world to the world she had visited in her dreams and on Valkrist . . . the magical world of her ancestors. Trembling all over, Emma cleared her throat, and then read the completed poem aloud:

> "You can't speak to me,
> but I can see it in your eyes—
> you understand exactly how I feel.

Nothing you could tell me
would come as a surprise.
I know your heart, so beautiful and real.

We run, and the world blurs
into streams of colored light.
My troubles fall behind and disappear.

You're with me in my dreams,
and it feels so true and right.
Anything can happen when you're near.

When I'm with you,
I'm strong and free—
and I know there's more
I'm supposed to be.

I don't know how,
and I don't know why,
but you give me wings,
and with wings I can fly!

Sometimes I get restless,
and I think I've lost my mind.
I don't know what I'm trying so hard to do.

But no matter what fate brings us,
I know I'm going to find
we can handle it together, me and you.

When I'm with you,
I'm strong and free,
and I know we'll find our destiny.

Come with me,
and we'll claim the sky,
because you give me wings,
and with wings I can fly."

When Emma had spoken the final word, the foal shuddered beside her. He shook his legs, and then let out a surprisingly strong whinny. Emma stroked his mane as his terrible wound shrank. The cut faded, until all that was left was his soft, silvery-white coat where the injury had been.

Emma climbed to her feet as the foal blinked his eyes and then rocked onto his chest. He struggled to stand up on his own hooves.

Then Emma's mouth dropped open as two downy silver wings sprang out from his withers, unfolding against his back.

With tears streaming down her face, Emma stroked the foal's forehead, and he exhaled a puff of strong breath, nuzzling her hand with his muzzle. Emma felt a surge of love from the colt, a burst of energy that connected to something deep within her and made her want to sing out in joy. They now had a mysterious and wonderful bond that could never be broken.

"I'm going to name you Wings," she whispered.

The colt whinnied again, and Emma hugged him around his neck, sobbing with happiness into his silver mane.

With Wings, Emma knew that she could fly.

Go to
www.bellasara.com
and enter the webcode below.
Enjoy!

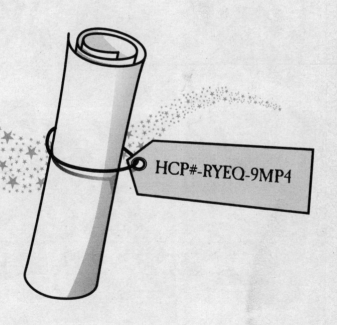

HCP#-RYEQ-9MP4